RHYMES FOR CHILDREN

Blushing Rose Publishing

Designed by Roni Akmon

Compiled By Nancy Akmon

Illustrations by Jessie Wilcox Smith,
Frederick Richardson, & M.T. Ross. Text by Betty Sage,
Edith Brown Kirkwood, & Mother Goose

Efforts have been made to find the copyright holders of material used in this publication.
We apologize for any omissions or errors and will be pleased to include the
appropriate acknowledgements in future editions.

ISBN# 1-884807-43-7

Blushing Rose Publishing
P.O. Box 2238
San Anselmo, Ca. 94979
www.blushingrose.com

Printed and bound in China

What are little boys made of ?
What are little boys made of ?
Frogs and snails
And puppy dog's tails,
That's what little boys are made of.

What are little girls made of?
What are little girls made of ?
Sugar and spice and everything nice,
That's what little girls are made of.

There was a little girl,
and she had a little curl
Right in the middle
of her forehead;
When she was good,
she was very, very good,
But when she was bad,
she was horrid.

JESSIE WILLCOX SMITH.

When Daddy was a little boy,
All little boys were good,
And did just what their parents
said they should;
And sometimes when I'm naughty
He takes me on his knee,
And tells me, when he was little,
How good he used to be.

The Cheetah is a
great big cat
But very quick,
for all of that,
She's cunning but
She's gentle, too,
And if you're good
she's good to you.

A dainty, and
fastidious man
is Lord Otter
Who can live just as
well on land as in water,
He'll eat but the
flakiest part of a fish,
And this he considers
his favorite dish.

Mary, Mary, quite contrary,
How does your garden grow?
With silver bells and cockle shells,
And pretty maids all in a row.

Ring around the rosie,
A pocket full of posies,
Ashes, ashes,
We all fall down!

She is dainty as snowdrops that fall from the skies,
Is this dear little Kitten with bright, shiny eyes
And velvety ears and pretty pink nose
And lovely white suit of soft, furry clothes.

Just look about and
see if you
Can find a friend
who's quite as true
As this old Doggie
that you see
A-smiling here
at you and me.

Mother told me once that bees wouldn't sting at all,

When they lit on my bare knees,-If I let them crawl, quietly,

without alarm, And didn't do them any harm.

Then Father said a funny thing-

That when bees *do* bite, - They leave behind their cruel sting,

Stuck in fast and tight. Of course, I always thought that then

They couldn't ever sting again.

The other day I saw one creeep- Right on Mother's frill,

Mother dear was fast asleep, So I kept very still,- The bee though,

must have got a scare, -For Mother nearly left her chair.

Then of course I had to find that bee to show to Dad,

And though his sting was left behind he bit him just as bad.

And so they both were wrong you see,

About the habits of the bee.

When young Mrs. Kangaroo goes for a hop, -To call or to market or, perhaps, out to shop, She has no nice carriage where baby can ride, - So he creeps in a pocket that hangs at her side.

When little
Miss Polar Bear
goes out to skate,
She never is bothered
by having to wait
Until mother wraps
her all snugly in fur,
For those are the
clothes that she
carries with her!

Hush-a-bye, Baby, upon the tree top,
When the wind blows the cradle will rock;
When the bough breaks the cradle will fall,
Down tumbles cradle and Baby and all.

Roses are red,
Violets are blue,
Sugar is sweet
And so are you.

He works on
tunnels night
and day,
This Marmot boy
from far away.
When winter comes
then he creeps,
And there until
spring he sleeps.